GILBERT

& THE SEARCH FOR THE LOST SMILE

WRITTEN BY KENNY LAMB
ILLUSTRATED BY JON BUCKNER

ISBN: 978-1-943978-21-2

Printed in China

CPSIA Tracking Label Information:
Production Location: Guangdong, China
Production Date: 4/15/2017
Cohort: Batch 68401

Library of Congress Cataloging-in-Publication Data available.

10 9 8 7 6 5 4 3 2 1

Written by Kenny Lamb
Illustrated by Jon Buckner

Produced by
Persnickety Press
120A North Salem Street
Apex, NC 27502

www.Persnickety-Press.com

GILBERt tHE GRUMP HAD LOSt HIS SMILE.

HE LOOKED UNDER THE BED...

AND BEHIND THE CHAIR

HE WENT UP TO THE ATTIC.

SO HE WENT to THE CREEK,
HIS FAVORIte PLACE.

HOPING to FIND
A SMILE FOR HIS FACE.

HE SWAM BY A FISH
WITH BLUE SPOTTED FINS.

HE tRIED SKIPPING ROCKS,
StILL NO SMILE tO SPARE...

HIS MOTHER AND FATHER MADE HIM A CAKE.

BUT WHEN IT WAS DONE
AND THE ICING WAS ON.

SO THEY ALL WENT OUTSIDE AND LOOKED REALLY HARD.

THEN GILBERT CLIMBED UP TO THE TOP OF THE TREE,
TO FIND WHAT HE'D FIND AND SEE WHAT HE'D SEE.